THE SILENT PULSE

Book 1

TONYA JONES

Copyright © 2025 Tonya Jones

All rights reserved.

No part of this publication may be reproduced, distributed, or transmitted in any form or by any means, including photocopying, recording, or other electronic or mechanical methods, without the prior written permission of the publisher, except in the case of brief quotations embodied in critical reviews and certain other noncommercial uses permitted by copyright law. For permission requests, email the publisher:

Attention: Permissions Coordinator

Welcome To The Storm Publishing!

info@w2tspublishing.net

Ordering Information:

Quantity sales. Special discounts are available on quantity purchases by corporations, associations, and others. For details, contact the publisher at the email address above.

Orders by U.S. trade bookstores and wholesalers.

Library of Congress Control Number: 2025923657 ISBN: 978-1-966612-88-9

Cover Design: Olaniyan Bukola

Austin Stephens, Austin S. Editing

First Printed Edition: December 2025

Printed in the United States of America

DEDICATION

For my beloved son, DJ: Your light continues to guide my every step. Though your voice is silent, your spirit speaks in every heartbeat of my life. This book, like every story I tell, carries your love within its pages.

For my precious grandson, Terrion: You are the living reflection of your father's love, a reminder that his legacy continues through your smile, your strength, and your heart. May you always walk in faith, knowing how deeply you are loved.

To my family: Thank you for standing beside me through every storm and every sunrise. Your love gives me courage, and your faith keeps me grounded.

And most of all, to God: All glory, honor, and praise. Without His grace, this journey would not be possible. Every word I write, every purpose fulfilled, is for His glory.

Table of Contents

AUTHOR NOTES

I define success as an author by completing the process. For me, success begins the moment God gives me an idea and I follow it through to the end. Writing the book, refining it, and finally holding it in my hands— that is the true accomplishment. I can't let sales or outside validation define me, because the real reward is being obedient to what God called me to do.

With this third book, that truth is even clearer. In a world focused on numbers and recognition, it's easy to let worth be tied to things we can't control. But the real victory is showing up every day, pushing through doubt, and trusting that every word serves a purpose. If even one reader feels seen, encouraged, or inspired by my work, then I've succeeded.

Of course, I have dreams beyond the page, book clubs discussing my work, author tours, making a bestseller list, or even a movie adaptation someday. Those would be incredible blessings. But I now understand they are not the foundation; they are the overflow.

The deepest fulfillment comes from knowing I found my voice again and had the courage to use it. That obedience and faithfulness to my calling is what defines true success for me.

INTRODUCTION

Every hospital has a heartbeat. Some are steady. Predictable. Safe. But St. Victoria Medical Center beats differently.

Its pulse is quick, strained, and irregular, like a secret trying too hard to stay hidden.

Behind these polished hallways and gleaming surgical suites, lives can be saved with a single decision... or lost in the shadow of one. Every beep of a monitor, every frantic footstep, every whispered conversation after midnight has a consequence. And in a place built on trust, the smallest lie can collapse everything.

This is the story of what happens when that trust fractures.

When a brilliant surgeon's steady hands begin to tremble. When a nurse who sees too much starts asking the wrong questions. When the board that claims to protect the hospital is the very thing poisoning it from within. And when a threat doesn't come with a face— but with a message, a warning, a countdown.

Whispers drift through the corridors. Unexplained shortages. Missing funds. Suspicious orders. Strange signatures. And someone—someone no one ever suspected—is pulling strings in the dark.

If you listen closely, you can hear it beneath the alarms and footsteps: a faint, irregular rhythm. A silent pulse.

It's the sound of lies tightening. Secrets unraveling. And danger creeping closer with every chapter.

In *The Silent Pulse: Whispers of Deceit*, the truth doesn't wait patiently. It stalks. It corners. It bleeds. And once it starts... no one—not the surgeon fighting his own demons, not the nurse uncovering a trail that shouldn't exist, not the board desperate to maintain their flawless image—is safe from what comes next.

So, take a breath. Steady your nerves. The story you're about to enter is one of betrayal, pressure, and choices that can shatter lives. In these halls, nothing is by accident. Nothing is coincidence. And nothing... absolutely nothing... is what it seems.

Welcome to St. Victoria. Listen closely. Because the pulse you hear? It might not belong to the living.

CHAPTER 1

Shadows in the Operating Room

The sharp scent of antiseptic filled the air, mingling with the low hum of monitors and the steady beeping of a heart-rate machine. Dr. Marcus Rainer stood at the center of the operating room; his gloved hands poised above the patient's exposed abdomen. Overhead lights threw sharp shadows across his face, highlighting the strain beneath his composed expression.

"Scalpel," Marcus said, his voice steady but missing its usual assurance. A nurse placed the instrument in his hand without hesitation, their movements brisk and controlled.

The surgical team worked in near silence; a rhythm built from repetition and trust. Yet something felt different tonight. The air was heavier, charged with unspoken tension. Marcus glanced at the clock on the wall, its ticking echoing louder in his mind than it should have. His fingers tightened around the scalpel.

"Dr. Rainer, vitals are dropping," said Elena Martinez, the head nurse, her calm but urgent tone cutting through the air. She stood beside the patient, eyes darting between the monitors and Marcus's face.

"I see it," Marcus replied, his voice sharp and controlled. "Increase fluids. Prepare the crash cart—just in case."

Elena pressed her lips into a thin line but gave a quick nod, signaling to the nearest nurse to act. She noticed the faint tremor in Marcus's hand as he adjusted his position. It wasn't the first time she had seen it, and each time, her concern deepened.

The monitors erupted in alarm, their shrill sound slicing through the sterile quiet. The patient's heart rate dropped sharply, and the room shifted into controlled urgency.

"Damn it," Marcus muttered under his breath. "Starting compressions. Get the defibrillator ready!"

Elena moved quickly, her years of experience allowing her to anticipate every command. Marcus began chest compressions, his jaw tightening with a desperation he fought to conceal. Sweat gathered at his forehead, threatening to drip beneath his mask. His mind raced, chasing each beat he tried to draw from the patient's failing heart.

"Clear!" Marcus shouted, stepping back. The defibrillator paddles pressed against the patient's chest, releasing a surge of electricity that made the body jolt briefly off the table. Every gaze snapped to the monitor. Nothing.

"Again," Marcus ordered, his tone sharp with frustration.

"Clear!"

Another shock. This time, the heart monitor stuttered, then settled into a weak but steady rhythm. A collective breath escaped the surgical team, almost audible in the sudden stillness. Marcus stepped back, his shoulders dropping as relief passed through him.

"Vitals are stabilizing," Elena said, her tone calm but her gaze steady on Marcus. "We're not out of the woods yet, but it's a good sign."

"Good work, everyone," Marcus said, though his voice lacked the energy of genuine relief. He passed the scalpel to a nurse and moved away from the operating table, his motions slower than usual.

Elena watched him peel off his gloves and leave the room. The door swung closed behind him, and a quiet unease settled in her chest — whatever haunted Dr. Rainer wasn't staying in the operating room.

Marcus's Escape

Marcus leaned heavily against the sink in the surgeons' lounge, cold water running over his trembling hands. He stared into the mirror, his own reflection accusing him with bloodshot eyes and a pale, sweat-slicked face. The pressure on his chest was suffocating, an invisible hand tightening with each passing second.

You're slipping, Marcus. You're going to kill someone.

The voice in his head had been relentless, a constant companion for months. He closed his eyes, gripping the sink's edges until his knuckles whitened. The ache in his hands from the tremors hadn't eased, a harsh reminder of what he could no longer control.

The door creaked open, and Marcus snapped his head up, catching Elena's reflection in the mirror. Her expression was unreadable, but her presence alone made his stomach twist.

"Marcus," she said softly, letting go of the formality she always maintained in the operating room. "We need to talk."

"I'm fine," he said quickly—too quickly. He shut off the water and reached for a paper towel, avoiding her gaze.

"You're not," Elena countered, stepping closer. "You almost lost that patient tonight."

"But I didn't," Marcus shot back, his voice defensive. "And that's what matters, isn't it?"

Elena crossed her arms, her steady composure unshaken. "Not if it happens again. You can't keep pushing yourself like this."

He turned to face her, jaw tight. "What exactly are you accusing me of, Elena?"

"I'm not accusing you of anything," she said evenly. "I'm worried about you. And if you won't admit that something's wrong, then maybe it's time someone else does."

Her words cut through the air, sharp and unyielding. Marcus's breath hitched as he searched her face for any sign of hesitation. There was none.

"This conversation is over," he said at last, brushing past her toward the door. "And I'd appreciate it if you stayed out of my business."

Elena watched him leave, a pang of frustration and worry pressing at her. Whatever Marcus was hiding, it was only a matter of time before it came to light—and she wasn't sure anyone, least of all Marcus, was ready for the consequences.

CHAPTER 2

Cracks in the Foundation

The hospital lobby was a blur of motion and sound—phones ringing, voices paging doctors, patients hurriedly wheeled to their destinations. But for Dr. Marcus Rainer, the chaos outside felt distant compared to the storm inside his mind. He stood near the elevators, clutching his phone and scrolling through emails he barely noticed. Each buzz and ping seemed to mock him.

"Dr. Rainer!" A sharp voice cut through the din. Marcus looked up to see Victoria Langston, the hospital's legal counsel, striding toward him in her signature heels. Her tailored suit radiated authority, and the set of her jaw hinted at impatience.

"Victoria," Marcus said, keeping his voice neutral. "What can I do for you?"

"Not here," she said curtly, her gaze sweeping the lobby. "My office. Now."

Victoria's Office

Victoria's office was as intimidating as she was—sleek, minimalist, and devoid of warmth. Marcus stepped in reluctantly, the door clicking shut behind him.

"Take a seat," she said, motioning to the leather chair opposite her desk. He didn't move.

"What's this about?" he asked, his voice strained but firm.

Victoria folded her hands on the desk; her piercing eyes fixed on him. "Rumors. Whispers, really. About your performance."

Marcus's chest tightened. "Is this coming from Elena?"

"It doesn't matter where it's coming from," Victoria replied sharply. "What matters is how it's being perceived. The board can't afford another scandal, Marcus. Not after last year."

"I'm fine," he said, though the words felt hollow.

Victoria arched an eyebrow, her expression skeptical. "You're not. And if you keep ignoring it, you'll force my hand."

"Meaning?"

"Meaning," she said, her voice dropping to a dangerous tone, "I'll have to involve the board. They'll demand evaluations, oversight, maybe even suspension."

Marcus's fists clenched. "You think threatening me is the way to fix this?"

"I'm not threatening you," Victoria said evenly. "I'm protecting this hospital. And if that means protecting it from you, so be it."

The silence stretched taut between them, thick with unspoken challenges. Finally, Marcus pushed back from the desk.

"I'll handle it," he said, turning toward the door.

"See that you do," Victoria called after him, her voice cool but firm.

Elena's Investigation

Meanwhile, Elena Martinez sat in the break room, her laptop open, a deep frown etched on her face. She scrolled through medication logs, noting discrepancies she couldn't explain.

"Something doesn't add up," she muttered.

Jacob Wyatt, one of the newer nurses, entered with a tray of coffee cups. "You talking to yourself again, Martinez?"

"Maybe," Elena replied distractedly, her eyes never leaving the screen.

Jacob set a cup in front of her and leaned over her shoulder. "What's got you so focused?"

Elena hesitated, glancing at him. Jacob was eager and bright, a bit too naive for his own good, but his intentions were genuine. She decided to test the waters.

"These med logs," she said, tilting the screen so he could see. "There's a pattern of shortages, but no explanation."

Jacob frowned. "Maybe inventory errors?"

"Maybe," Elena echoed. "Or maybe something worse."

Jacob's expression turned serious. "Worse, like... intentional?"

"I don't know yet," Elena admitted. "But if someone's tampering with the supply, it could explain a lot."

Jacob nodded slowly, his mind visibly turning over the implications. "You think Marcus knows about this?"

Elena pressed her lips into a thin line. "Marcus has enough on his plate. But we'll need answers soon—before someone else gets hurt."

Marcus's Private Struggles

That night, Marcus sat alone in his dimly lit apartment. A half-empty bottle of whiskey rested on the table beside him, the amber liquid catching the glow of a single lamp. His hands trembled as he scrolled through his phone, messages and calls from concerned colleagues and friends left unanswered.

A photo on the wall caught his eye: a younger version of himself, grinning and confident, surrounded by his surgical team after a successful procedure. The man in the photo felt like a stranger.

You're not that man anymore, he thought bitterly. And you never will be.

His phone buzzed, breaking the silence. A text from an unknown number appeared on the screen.

Message: We know what you've done. Time's running out.

Marcus's breath caught as he stared at the screen. The message glared back at him, its meaning sinking in like a slow toxin. His pulse quickened, and the room seemed to shrink around him. Whoever had sent that text knew something—something he couldn't afford to let come to light.

He drained the last of his whiskey in one swallow, the burn doing nothing to steady his nerves. Setting the glass down, his hand trembled despite his effort to control it. The silence in the room pressed against him, amplifying the pounding in his chest. Whatever game had begun, the stakes had just risen—and Marcus was running out of time to stop everything from collapsing.

CHAPTER 3

Shadows of Suspicion

The first rays of dawn slipped through the blinds of the hospital break room, washing over the worn leather couches and the half-empty coffee cups scattered across the table. Elena Martinez sat in her usual spot, the bluish glow of her laptop screen accentuating the fatigue etched into her face. She'd spent most of the night combing through the medication logs, her unease deepening with each inconsistency she found.

Leaning back in her chair, she rubbed her temples. What am I missing? The numbers didn't lie. Something was wrong—and it wasn't a simple inventory mistake.

The door creaked open, breaking her concentration. Jacob Wyatt stepped in, balancing a box of donuts in one hand and two steaming cups of coffee in the other. His easy smile faltered when he noticed the strain in Elena's expression.

"You're still at it?" he asked, setting the box and one of the cups in front of her.

"Couldn't sleep," Elena said, accepting the coffee with a faint smile. "Thanks."

"You're going to burn out if you keep this up," Jacob said, pulling up a chair. "What's so important that it's keeping you here all night?"

Elena hesitated, her fingers tapping the edge of her laptop. She'd already shared her suspicions with Jacob yesterday, but now that she'd uncovered more, she wasn't sure how much further to go.

"The shortages," she said finally, turning the laptop toward him. "They're not random. Look at this." She pointed to a series of dates and amounts. "All these discrepancies trace back to the same account—one tied to the hospital's research fund."

Jacob's brow furrowed as he studied the data. "That... doesn't look good. Do you think it's deliberate?"

"I'm not sure yet," Elena said, leaning forward. "But if it is, whoever's responsible has worked hard to cover their tracks."

Marcus's Morning

Dr. Marcus Rainer's morning started with a sudden buzz—not from his alarm clock, but from his phone vibrating on the nightstand. He groaned, squinting against the sunlight filtering through the blinds as he reached for it. On the screen, a notification from an unknown number flashed back at him.

Message: Tick tock, Marcus. Time's running out.

Marcus's stomach churned. The messages had started a week ago—each one more unsettling than the last. At first, he'd convinced himself they were a prank, but after last night's text—and the relentless voice that never left his head—they were impossible to ignore.

He sat up, dragging a hand through his disheveled hair. The half-empty whiskey bottle from the night before sat on the table, the untouched glass beside it catching the morning light. Marcus reached for it, then hesitated, his hand frozen midair.

With a quiet exhale, he let it fall back to his side and picked up his phone instead. Scrolling through the hospital directory, he stopped at one name.

"Elena," he murmured under his breath, thumb hovering over the call button.

A long pause. Then he sighed and tossed the phone onto the couch. No. I'll handle this myself.

Elena and Victoria Cross Paths

Elena had just finished updating Jacob on her findings when Victoria Langston walked into the break room. As always, the hospital's legal counsel looked perfectly composed, her heels clicking against the tiled floor with a confidence that demanded attention.

"Nurse Martinez," Victoria said, her tone smooth and measured. "A word?"

Elena's stomach tightened. She'd been expecting this. Victoria's sudden appearances rarely meant anything good, and the last thing Elena needed was more scrutiny.

"Of course," she replied, keeping her expression neutral as she followed Victoria into the hallway.

They stopped near the elevators, away from passing staff. Victoria's gaze studied Elena's face for a long moment before she finally spoke.

"You've been asking questions," she said quietly, her voice steady but firm. "Questions that could lead to… complications."

Elena folded her arms, refusing to be intimidated. "If you're referring to the medication discrepancies, I'm just trying to make sure patients are safe."

"Is that all?" Victoria's gaze sharpened. "Because the board doesn't take kindly to baseless accusations."

Elena's shoulders stiffened. "I haven't made any accusations. Yet."

Victoria's lips curved into a faint smile that never touched her eyes. "Good. Let's keep it that way—for your sake."

The elevator chimed, its doors sliding open. Victoria stepped inside without another word, leaving Elena alone in the hallway. A chill crept over her, sinking beneath her composure. Whatever was happening at St. Victoria Medical Center, it was bigger—and far more dangerous—than she'd realized.

Message: Rainer's slipping. Martinez is digging too deep. Handle it.

The figure smirked, typing a quick reply.

Response: Already in progress.

The camera lingered on the monitor as the figure's hand reached for a coffee cup, the words "St. Victoria Medical Center" emblazoned on its side. A single keystroke sent the copied files into cyberspace, their destination unknown.

CHAPTER 4

Secrets in Plain Sight

The rain pounded against the windows of St. Victoria Medical Center, a steady rhythm that echoed the tension simmering inside its walls.

Elena Martinez stood at the nurses' station, leaning against the counter with a clipboard in hand. Her gaze was unfocused, her thoughts far from the routine updates she was supposed to be recording. Every discrepancy she'd found in the medication logs replayed in her mind, each one sounding more like a warning she couldn't ignore.

"Earth to Elena," Jacob Wyatt said, snapping her out of her trance. He stood beside her with a file folder tucked under one arm. "You look like you've seen a ghost."

"Maybe I have," she muttered, taking the file from him. She flipped it open, but the words blurred together on the page.

Jacob frowned. "You've been off all morning. Is this about... you know?"

Elena glanced around to make sure they were alone. "I can't stop thinking about it. Every time I try to connect the dots, something new comes up."

Jacob raised an eyebrow. "Like what?"

She hesitated, then lowered her voice. "Like this."

She turned to the nearby computer and pulled up a series of recent transactions linked to the hospital's research fund. "These payments don't make sense. The amounts are too large for standard expenses, and the money's being routed into an account I can't trace."

Jacob leaned in, his brow furrowing. "Are you saying someone's stealing from the hospital?"

"I'm saying something's off," Elena replied. "And I'm starting to think it ties back to the shortages."

Marcus's Confrontation

Dr. Marcus Rainer's day wasn't going any better. He paced across his office, the walls seeming to close in on him. The cryptic texts, the mounting pressure, and now Elena's questions—it was too much. He was mid-stride when the door burst open.

"Dr. Rainer," Victoria Langston entered, her expression caught between irritation and concern. "We need to talk."

"I don't have time for this," Marcus said sharply, but Victoria's glare stopped him in his tracks.

"Make time," she replied, closing the door behind her. "Do you know how many complaints have crossed my desk this week?"

Marcus sighed, running a hand through his hair. "I'm doing my best, Victoria."

"Your best isn't enough," she shot back. "The hospital's already under scrutiny, and your behavior isn't helping."

"My behavior?" Marcus's voice rose. "You think I'm the problem? What about the real issues no one seems willing to face?"

Victoria's eyes narrowed. "If you're implying something, Marcus, you'd better be prepared to back it up."

He opened his mouth to reply but stopped himself. The stakes were too high, and Victoria was the last person he could trust. "Forget it," he muttered, turning away. "This conversation is over."

"For now," Victoria said coldly, letting the door slam behind her as she left.

Unlikely Alliances

Elena and Jacob's investigation led them to the hospital archives: a dimly lit room lined with rows of filing cabinets and piles of dusty paperwork. The rain tapping against the roof was their only companion as they sifted through the records.

"This feels like a scene from a bad crime show," Jacob joked, holding up a file labeled Research Grants.

"If this were a crime show, we'd have found the smoking gun by now," Elena replied flatly. She flipped through another file, pausing when something caught her eye. "Wait a second."

Jacob leaned over her shoulder. "What is it?"

Elena pointed to a series of grants awarded to the hospital's research division. "These amounts match the payments I found earlier. But look at the signatures."

Jacob squinted at the documents. "Dr. Rainer?"

Elena nodded. "If these records are accurate, Marcus approved every single one of these grants."

A Quiet Admission

Elena's discovery led her to Marcus's office later that evening. She knocked hesitantly, half hoping he wouldn't answer. The door creaked open, and Marcus stood there, his expression weary.

"Elena," he said, stepping aside. "What can I do for you?"

She held up the file, her heart pounding. "I need to know the truth... about these grants."

Marcus froze, eyes darting to the folder in her hand. He closed the door slowly, the tension in the room tightening.

"Where did you get that?" he asked quietly.

"It doesn't matter," Elena replied. "What matters is whether these signatures are yours."

Marcus sank into his chair, rubbing his temples. The weight of his secrets pressed down on him. "Yes," he admitted finally. "They're mine."

Elena's stomach dropped. "Why? Marcus... what are you involved in?"

"It's not what you think," he said quickly. "I didn't steal anything. But I… I was pressured into signing those grants. I didn't ask questions, and I should have."

"Who pressured you?" Elena demanded.

Marcus hesitated, then shook his head. "I can't. Not yet."

"You're running out of time, Marcus," Elena said, frustration edging her voice. "If you don't come clean, someone else will."

Closing Scene

In the shadows of the hospital's parking lot, the antagonist watched as Elena left Marcus's office, her expression grim. They smirked, pulling out their phone and typing a message.

Message: They're getting closer. Time to escalate.

The rain continued to fall as the figure slipped into the night, their next move already in motion.

CHAPTER 5

Beneath the Surface

The fluorescent lights in the hospital staff lounge flickered, casting a wavering glow over the room. Elena Martinez sat alone at a corner table, her fingers drumming against the surface as she stared at her phone. Last night's confrontation with Marcus had left her restless, and the revelations in the file weighed heavily on her mind.

Her thoughts were interrupted when Jacob Wyatt entered, balancing a tray with two coffees. He slid one toward her and took a seat.

"You look like you didn't sleep," he said, his tone light but edged with concern.

Elena smirked faintly. "That obvious?"

"You've got the classic signs," Jacob said, gesturing to the dark circles under her eyes. "Care to share what's keeping you up?"

She hesitated, then sighed. "It's Marcus. I talked to him about the grants."

Jacob leaned forward, curiosity sharpening his features. "And? What did he say?"

Elena lowered her voice. "He admitted to signing off on them. But he says he was pressured into it... he wouldn't say by whom."

Jacob's brow furrowed. "Do you believe him?"

Elena shrugged. "I don't know. But if he's telling the truth, it means someone higher up is pulling the strings."

Marcus's Attempt to Cope

Meanwhile, Dr. Marcus Rainer stood in the operating room—not performing surgery but staring at the empty table. The sterile scent of antiseptic filled the air, mingling with the churn of his thoughts.

You're losing it, he thought bitterly. They're going to find out, and when they do...

"Dr. Rainer?"

The voice startled him. He turned to see a junior surgeon standing hesitantly in the doorway.

"The board is asking for an update on your patient from last night," the surgeon said. "They... seem concerned about the complications."

Marcus's stomach twisted, but he nodded curtly. "I'll handle it."

After the surgeon left, Marcus leaned against the counter, gripping its edge until his knuckles turned white. The weight of the board's scrutiny pressed down on him, and with Victoria breathing down his neck, he knew his time was running out.

Victoria's Calculations

In her corner office overlooking the city, Victoria Langston sat behind her desk, flipping through a stack of documents. Her eyes scanned each page with precision, noting discrepancies that mirrored the ones Elena had uncovered.

Her phone buzzed. She glanced at the screen—a message from an unknown number.

Message: Martinez and Wyatt are digging too deep. Rainer is unstable. Do something.

Victoria's jaw tightened. She picked up the phone and dialed a number, her voice sharp when the line connected.

"We have a problem," she said. "A big one. Meet me tonight."

She ended the call, her mind already racing through strategies. If the hospital's secrets unraveled, she would make sure she wasn't left holding the pieces.

A Dangerous Discovery

Back in the archives, Elena and Jacob sifted through another set of files. The dim light and the musty smell of old paper made the room feel heavier.

"This is useless," Jacob muttered, slamming a folder shut. "It's like they've buried anything incriminating under a mountain of bureaucracy."

Elena paused, her eyes locking onto a single sheet of paper. "Not everything," she said, holding it up. "Look at this."

Jacob leaned over her shoulder, brow furrowed. The document detailed a transfer of funds from the hospital's research account to an offshore account under a name neither of them recognized.

"That's... suspicious," Jacob said.

"Suspicious enough to be dangerous," Elena replied. "Whoever's behind this went to great lengths to hide it."

Jacob hesitated. "You think this connects back to Marcus?"

"Maybe," Elena said. "But I think it goes further than him."

Closing Scene

That night, Marcus sat in his dimly lit apartment, nursing a glass of water. The messages had stopped—for now—but the silence pressed in, heavier than any warning. He stared at the file Elena had confronted him with earlier, the names and numbers merging into a blur.

His phone buzzed. He picked it up warily. On the screen, a single word glared back at him.

Message: Run.

A chill ran down his spine as he stared at the word. Outside, a car's headlights briefly illuminated his living room before disappearing into the night. Marcus set the phone down with trembling hands, knowing that whatever game he was caught in, it was about to escalate.

CHAPTER 6

Through Shadows and Doubts

The morning light filtered weakly through the blinds of the hospital cafeteria, casting faint lines across the empty tables. Elena Martinez sat in a corner, absently stirring a cup of coffee that had long gone cold. Across from her, Jacob Wyatt leaned forward, arms folded on the table, his expression a mix of curiosity and concern.

"So, let me get this straight," Jacob said, keeping his voice low. "Marcus admitted to signing the grants but claims he was pressured into it. By whom?"

Elena shook her head. "He wouldn't say. But if he's telling the truth, someone higher up is pulling the strings."

Jacob frowned. "Higher up? You mean the board?"

"Maybe," Elena said, her tone uncertain. "Or someone with enough power to make Marcus follow orders without question. Whoever it is, they've covered their tracks well."

Jacob leaned back in his chair, thinking. "We need more evidence. Something solid that ties all of this together."

"Easier said than done," Elena muttered, her gaze flicking toward the cafeteria door. Her stomach tightened. The deeper they went, the more dangerous it became.

Victoria's Warning

In her office, Victoria Langston sat behind her polished desk, her sharp gaze fixed on Marcus Rainer. He stood before her, arms crossed, expression guarded.

"You're coming apart, Marcus," Victoria said, her tone cold and controlled. "If you don't get a grip, you're going to take the rest of us down with you."

Marcus's jaw tightened. "Is that a threat?"

"It's a fact," Victoria snapped. "The board is already asking questions, and Elena Martinez isn't as discreet as she thinks. If she finds something that links back to you, it's game over."

"I'm not the one she should be worried about," Marcus retorted. "Why don't you tell me who really benefits from those grants?"

Victoria's eyes narrowed. "Be careful, Marcus. You're treading on dangerous ground."

A Meeting in the Shadows

That evening, Elena and Jacob met in a secluded corner of the hospital archives. The air smelled of old paper and faint mildew, and the dim light threw uneven shadows across the walls.

"I found something," Jacob said, handing her a folder. "It's a series of emails between the research department and someone offsite. The sender's name is redacted but look at the tone."

Elena flipped through the pages, her pulse quickening. The messages were cryptic but deliberate, referencing "additional resources" and "necessary discretion."

"This proves someone's pulling the strings," she said quietly. "But it's not enough. We need names."

"Then we keep looking," Jacob replied. "But we'd better be careful. Whoever's behind this won't let us search forever."

Marcus's Breaking Point

Marcus sat in his darkened apartment, a single lamp casting a pool of light over the scattered documents before him. His hands trembled as he sifted through them, the weight of his secrets pressing heavily on his chest.

His phone buzzed. He picked it up with a weary sigh. Another message from an unknown number.

Message: Time's up. Act, or we will.

Marcus slammed the phone down, his breath coming in shallow gasps. The walls felt like they were closing in, the room spinning around him. He buried his face in his hands, the pressure finally breaking through his defenses.

You can't keep running, he thought. *But if you stop, they'll destroy you.*

The Antagonist's Move

In a dimly lit office across the city, a shadowy figure typed furiously on a laptop. The screen's glow reflected off their glasses as they worked, sending encrypted messages and preparing for the next phase of their plan.

A phone buzzed on the desk. The figure glanced at the notification, their fingers hovering over the keys.

Message: Martinez and Wyatt are close. Neutralize them.

The figure smirked, typing a quick reply.

Response: Consider it done.

They leaned back in their chair, the faint sound of rain against the window a soothing backdrop to their machinations. St. Victoria Medical Center was on the brink of collapse, and they were ready to light the final match.

Closing Scene

Elena and Jacob moved through the dimly lit parking garage, their voices barely above a whisper.

"We're getting close," Jacob said, clutching the folder tightly. "But I can't shake the feeling we're being watched."

Elena glanced over her shoulder, her instincts on high alert. The shadows seemed to shift with their steps; every sound echoed in the thick silence.

"Stay sharp," she murmured. "If someone's out there, they won't catch us off guard."

Unseen by them, a pair of eyes tracked their movements from the darkness. The figure stepped deeper into the shadows, a phone in hand—and a plan already in motion.

CHAPTER 7

The First Move

The air inside the conference room at St. Victoria Medical Center was charged with tension. The fluorescent lights buzzed softly, casting a cold, sterile glow over the group gathered around the long table. Elena Martinez and Jacob Wyatt sat side by side, their folders of evidence stacked neatly in front of them. Across the table, Victoria Langston leaned back in her chair, her sharp eyes fixed on Dr. Marcus Rainer, who stood at the head of the room.

"We can't keep this quiet," Marcus began, his voice steady but tight. "If we do, we're complicit in whatever's happening. We owe it to the staff, the patients, and ourselves to bring it out into the open."

Victoria's lips thinned. "Bringing it out doesn't solve the problem, Marcus. It creates chaos—lawsuits, funding cuts, and eventually the collapse of this hospital."

"And pretending nothing's wrong makes us better?" Jacob shot back, his tone sharper than he meant. "We've found evidence—clear evidence—that someone's funneling money and putting patients at risk. How is that acceptable?"

Victoria's gaze shifted to Jacob, her expression unreadable. "It's not about what's acceptable, Mr. Wyatt. It's about survival. If St. Victoria's reputation collapses, we all go down with it."

"So, we do nothing?" Elena cut in, her voice tight with frustration. "Let more people get hurt? Let more funds vanish? How does that help anyone?"

"Enough," Marcus said, raising a hand. His eyes swept the room, his expression hard. "We're not here to argue—we're here to decide how to move forward."

The Proposal

Elena took a deep breath and opened one of the folders in front of her. She slid a printed email toward the center of the table.

"This is a communication between the research department and an offshore account holder," she said. "The account is tied to several questionable transactions, all approved under Dr. Rainer's name. But the funds...

they're not being used for research. They're being funneled into private accounts."

Victoria's eyes flicked to Marcus, who stayed silent, his jaw tight.

"And you think going public with this is the best move?" she asked.

Jacob shook his head. "Not yet. First, we bring it to the board. We show them the evidence and demand accountability. If they ignore it, then we go public."

"And if the board strikes back?" Victoria pressed. "If they fire you—or blacklist you?"

Jacob's voice stayed steady. "Then at least we'll know we didn't look the other way."

A Heated Confrontation

Later that afternoon, the group stood before the hospital's board of directors. The large, wood-paneled room felt imposing, portraits of past directors glaring down from the walls.

Marcus led the presentation, his voice steady though his hands trembled slightly as he outlined the evidence.

"These transactions compromise the integrity of this institution," he finished. "If we don't act now, it'll only get worse."

One of the board members—an older man with silver hair and a sharp gaze—leaned forward.

"And what do you suggest we do, Dr. Rainer? Tear apart the research department? Launch a public investigation? You're asking us to destroy our own credibility."

"No," Elena said, stepping closer to the table. "We're asking you to stop the corruption before it destroys this hospital from the inside out."

The room fell into a tense silence, the weight of her words hanging heavy over everyone.

An Unlikely Ally

As the meeting adjourned, Marcus stayed behind, his thoughts in turmoil. Victoria crossed the room, her expression unexpectedly soft.

"You're playing a dangerous game, Marcus," she said quietly.

"I don't have a choice," he replied, voice flat with fatigue. "None of us do."

Victoria hesitated, then let out a soft sigh. "If you're going to do this, you'll need leverage. I might have something that can help."

Marcus's eyes narrowed. "Why would you help me?"

Victoria's mouth tilted into a faint smile. "Because if this hospital goes down, so do I. I won't let that happen."

The Antagonist's Move

In the shadows of the hospital's parking garage, a figure sat in a sleek, black car, their phone glowing faintly in the darkness. They typed a message, their fingers flying over the screen.

Message: They've gone to the board. Time to accelerate the plan.

The message sent, the figure leaned back, their face obscured by shadows. The faint sound of footsteps echoed through the garage, and the figure's eyes followed a pair of silhouettes disappearing into the stairwell. A slow, calculated smile spread across their face.

Closing Scene

Elena, Jacob, and Marcus gathered in the staff lounge, the day's events weighing heavily on them.

"Do you think the board will act?" Jacob asked, his voice threaded with equal parts hope and doubt.

"They'll have to," Marcus replied, but the conviction was missing from his tone.

Elena stared out at the city beyond the windows, jaw set. "If they don't, we'll make sure the public learns what's really going on."

Outside, the city lights blinked against the dark sky — a quiet counterpoint to the storm building inside St. Victoria Medical Center.

CHAPTER 8

The Weight of Legacy

The quiet hum of the hospital carried the weight of unspoken emotions. The air felt heavy, thick with anticipation, regret, and the sense that change was coming. For Marcus, the day began like any other: rushing between surgeries, meetings, and endless paperwork. Yet beneath the surface, a storm was brewing—one he could no longer ignore.

A Meeting with Elena

Elena Martinez had spent most of the morning reviewing patient files and following up on the discrepancies she and Jacob had uncovered. Each discovery painted an increasingly damning picture of the hospital's hidden operations, and the stakes had never been higher. By the time she sought out Marcus, her determination was unwavering.

She found him in his office, staring out the window at the city skyline.

"Marcus," she said, her tone sharper than usual, "we need to talk."

He turned, his expression guarded. "About what?"

Elena closed the door behind her and crossed her arms. "About the grants. The medication shortages. And whatever else you've been keeping from us."

Marcus sighed, running a hand through his hair. "I told you—I signed the grants, but I didn't know what they were really funding. I was pressured into it."

"And who pressured you?" Elena demanded. "You keep dodging that question, but we're running out of time, Marcus. If we don't act soon, it won't just be your reputation on the line—it'll be everyone's."

He sank into his chair, rubbing his temples. "It's not that simple. If I come forward without solid proof, they'll bury me. And they'll bury you too if they think you're involved."

"Then we find proof," Elena said firmly. "Together. But you have to start being honest with me. With all of us."

Marcus met her gaze, the weight of her words sinking in. Finally, he nodded. "Alright. Let's do this."

The Discovery

Elena and Marcus joined Jacob in the hospital archives later that day. The dimly lit room smelled of old paper, and the faint hum of fluorescent lights filled the space. Jacob was already poring over a stack of files when they arrived.

"Found anything?" Elena asked.

Jacob looked up, his expression grim. "Plenty. But this—" He handed Elena a file, his finger pointing to a line of transactions—"this is what caught my attention."

Elena scanned the document, her heart sinking. "Offshore accounts," she murmured. "And tied to the research division. This is bigger than we thought."

Marcus leaned over her shoulder, brow furrowed. "These amounts... they don't make sense. No single project could require that much funding."

"Exactly," Jacob said. "Someone's siphoning money, and they're using the hospital's reputation to cover their tracks."

Elena closed the file, her resolve hardening. "We need to take this to the board. They can't ignore it."

"They might," Marcus said, voice wary. "But it's worth a shot."

A Suspicious Interruption

As the trio left the archives, a voice called from behind them.

"Working late?"

They turned to see Victoria Langston, the hospital's legal counsel, her expression unreadable. Her heels clicked against the tiled floor as she approached.

"Just tying up some loose ends," Elena said evenly.

Victoria's gaze swept over them, lingering on the files in Elena's hands. "Be careful," she said, tone deceptively casual. "Sometimes, when you dig too deep, you find things you wish you hadn't."

Marcus stiffened, but Elena held her ground. "Thanks for the advice," she said. "We'll keep that in mind."

Victoria smiled faintly, though it didn't reach her eyes. "Goodnight." She walked away, leaving a ripple of unease behind.

A Private Moment

That night, Marcus sat in his apartment, the files spread across the desk. The evidence was damning, and he knew it was only a matter of time before everything came to light. Yet his thoughts kept returning to Daniel—the son he had lost, and the legacy he had failed to protect.

Reaching for his desk drawer, Marcus pulled out an old photograph of Daniel as a child, his face alight with joy.

"I'm trying, son," Marcus whispered, voice thick with emotion. "I'm trying to make it right."

His phone buzzed, breaking the silence. A message had arrived from an unknown number.

You're running out of time.

Marcus's hand trembled as he read the words. The walls seemed to close in around him, the weight of his secrets threatening to crush him. But beneath the fear, a flicker of determination burned. He wasn't ready to give up—not yet.

Closing Scene

The day's events sent ripples that would carry into the next chapter. Marcus's renewed determination to uncover the truth, coupled with Elena and Jacob's growing resolve, set the stage for the battles ahead. Together, they would confront the storm brewing within St. Victoria Medical Center — whether they were ready or not.

CHAPTER 9

Through His Son's Eyes

The office was quiet, broken only by the soft ticking of a wall clock. Marcus sat alone at his desk, clutching a photo frame tightly. The picture showed a younger version of himself standing beside his son, Daniel, outside the hospital on a bright spring day. The boy's grin was infectious, his eyes shining with pride as he looked up at his father.

What would he think of me now? Marcus wondered, his grip tightening on the frame.

A Memory Rekindled

Marcus's thoughts drifted back to the day the photo was taken. Daniel had visited the hospital as part of a school project, shadowing his father for a day. The boy had been fascinated by everything—the bustling hallways, the whirring machines, the life-and-death urgency of the operating room.

"Will I be a doctor like you someday, Dad?" Daniel had asked, his voice full of wonder.

"If that's what you want," Marcus had replied, ruffling his son's hair. "But whatever you choose, make sure it's something you're proud of."

The memory was bittersweet now. Marcus had always tried to live up to those words, but the past few months had made him question whether he had.

Elena's Observation

Later that day, Elena found Marcus sitting in the hospital courtyard, the photo frame resting on the bench beside him. She hesitated, sensing he was lost in thought.

"You okay?" she asked gently.

Marcus looked up, startled, and offered a faint smile, gesturing for her to sit. "Just... remembering," he said, nodding toward the photo. "That's my son, Daniel."

Elena picked up the frame, studying the picture. "He looks a lot like you," she said. "How old would he be now?"

"He... would have been twenty-five," Marcus said quietly, his voice tinged with sadness. "He passed away a few years ago."

Elena's breath caught. "Marcus, I'm so sorry. I didn't know."

"It's okay," Marcus replied, his gaze distant. "Daniel was the reason I wanted to be better. To set an example. But somewhere along the way, I lost sight of that."

"Maybe this is your chance to find it again," Elena said softly.

Marcus met her eyes, the weight of her words settling over him. "Maybe," he said.

A Letter from the Past

That evening, Marcus returned to his apartment. As he rummaged through a drawer searching for a file, his fingers brushed against an old envelope with Daniel's handwriting on the front. His chest tightened as he opened it, revealing a letter his son had written years ago for a school assignment.

Dear Dad,

You're my hero. I know you work a lot and sometimes miss my games, but I understand. You save people's lives, and that's the most important thing. Someday, I want to be like you— someone who helps others and makes the world a better place.

Love, Daniel

Marcus's hands shook as he read the letter. Tears blurred his vision, but a sense of clarity began to take hold. He folded the letter carefully and placed it back in the envelope, his resolve hardening.

It's time to be the man he believed I was.

Renewed Purpose

The next morning, Marcus arrived at the hospital earlier than usual. He met Elena and Jacob in the staff lounge, his expression set with determination.

"I've been thinking," he said. "We've been so focused on exposing what's wrong here that we've lost sight of why we're fighting."

Elena and Jacob exchanged a glance, then nodded for him to continue.

"This hospital has always been more than just a building," Marcus said. "It's a place where lives are saved, where people find hope. That's what we need to protect—not just from corruption, but from ourselves."

"So, what do we do?" Jacob asked.

"We remind everyone why we're here," Marcus replied. "We rally the staff, bring them together. If we stand united, we can rebuild trust—not just in the hospital, but in each other."

Closing Scene

As the day drew to a close, Marcus stood at the hospital entrance, watching staff and patients move through the lobby. Daniel's letter rested in his pocket, a quiet reminder of the legacy he wanted to honor.

Behind him, Elena and Jacob joined him, their presence a steady reassurance.

"You ready for this?" Elena asked.

Marcus nodded. "I have to be. For him."

Together, they stepped back into the hospital, carrying the weight of their mission tempered by the hope they held.

CHAPTER 10

The Silent Pulse

The sound of applause echoed through the grand ballroom of St. Victoria Medical Center. The annual charity gala, celebrating the hospital's achievements and raising funds for future projects, was a dazzling affair. Crystal chandeliers cast a warm glow across the room, highlighting guests in elegant attire. Yet beneath the champagne toasts and polite conversation, tension simmered.

Marcus Rainer stood near the edge of the room, nursing a glass of water and scanning the crowd. His earlier optimism had dimmed; the faces around him were a mix of genuine supporters and those likely hiding something.

"Quite the turnout," Elena Martinez said, stepping up beside him. She wore a simple black dress—understated yet elegant—her usual no-nonsense demeanor softened for the occasion.

"Yeah," Marcus replied, his eyes fixed on a group of board members laughing near the bar. "Let's just hope it's more than a show."

Elena followed his gaze, her expression tightening. "You think they'll make a move tonight?"

"If they do, we'll be ready," Marcus said firmly. "This isn't just about exposing the truth anymore. It's about taking back control.

The Plan in Motion

At a table near the stage, Jacob Wyatt adjusted his bow tie, nerves evident in the slight tremor of his hands. In front of him, a small recording device rested discreetly under a folded napkin. He glanced across the room at Elena, who gave him a subtle nod.

The plan was simple: capture any incriminating conversations between key players. The gala's atmosphere of camaraderie could lower guards, giving them the chance to gather the evidence they desperately needed.

As the program began, the room quieted. Victoria Langston took the stage, her presence commanding as she addressed the crowd.

"Ladies and gentlemen, thank you for joining us tonight," she began, her polished tone masking the tension beneath. "St. Victoria Medical Center has always been a beacon of hope, a place where miracles happen every day. But none of this would be possible without your support."

Polite applause filled the room, though Marcus's hands remained still. He exchanged a glance with Elena, who looked equally unimpressed.

An Unexpected Revelation

As the evening wore on, Marcus found himself cornered by one of the board members, a man named Richard Hayes. Hayes's smile was too wide, his handshake unnervingly firm.

"Dr. Rainer," Hayes said, his tone heavy with false camaraderie. "Enjoying the gala?"

"It's... enlightening," Marcus replied cautiously.

Hayes chuckled, clapping Marcus on the shoulder. "Good, good. You know, we've all been very impressed with your work recently. Navigating the... challenges we've faced hasn't been easy."

Marcus's eyes narrowed. "Challenges like those outlined in the financial reports?"

For a fraction of a second, Hayes's smile wavered. Then he recovered, leaning in closer. "Now, now, Marcus. Let's not ruin a good evening with unpleasant topics. Why don't we focus on the future?"

Marcus's jaw tightened. "The future doesn't mean much if we can't confront the truth about the past."

Hayes's expression stiffened, but before he could respond, Elena appeared at Marcus's side.

"Everything okay here?" she asked, her voice calm but firm.

"Of course," Hayes said smoothly, stepping back. "Enjoy the evening."

As he disappeared into the crowd, Marcus exhaled sharply. "He knows something. They all do."

The Antagonist Strikes

Meanwhile, in a secluded corner of the ballroom, the orchestrator of the hospital's corruption watched the evening unfold with quiet amusement. Their eyes never left Marcus and Elena, noting the intensity of their conversation.

A phone buzzed in their hand, a new message flashing across the screen.

Message: Rainer and Martinez are getting too close. Handle it.

The antagonist typed a reply.

Response: Consider it done.

They slipped through the crowd unnoticed, their next move already in motion.

The Night Unravels

As the gala neared its conclusion, Victoria returned to the stage, her polished facade firmly in place.

"Before we end this wonderful evening, I'd like to thank everyone for their generosity and dedication to St. Victoria Medical Center," she said. "Together, we can continue to provide world-class care and innovation."

The applause was thunderous, but Marcus barely registered it. His attention was on Jacob, who offered a discreet thumbs-up. They had captured several conversations that could prove useful—including one between Hayes and another board member discussing "misplaced funds."

As the crowd began to disperse, Marcus's phone buzzed. The sender was unknown, but the message was unmistakably clear.

Message: You think you've won?

This is far from over.

Closing Scene

Outside the ballroom, Marcus, Elena, and Jacob gathered in the cool night air. The distant hum of city traffic filled the background as they reviewed the night's events.

"We got what we needed," Jacob said, holding up the recording device. "But it's not enough to take them down."

"Then we keep going," Elena replied, her tone firm. "We're closer than ever. They're scared, and that tells us we're on the right track."

Marcus nodded, his resolve solid. "Let's finish this."

From the shadows, the antagonist watched them, expression unreadable. The game was far from over, and the stakes had never been higher.

CHAPTER 11

The Fallout

The morning after the gala was subdued, the energy at St. Victoria Medical Center tense but focused. The stakes had never been higher, and Marcus Rainer felt it in every interaction, every glance cast his way. He sat in the break room with Elena Martinez and Jacob Wyatt, their expressions grim as they reviewed the recordings from the night before.

"This conversation is key," Jacob said, pointing to a timestamp on the laptop screen. The faint sound of Richard Hayes's voice crackled through the speakers, discussing "misplaced funds" and "strategic adjustments."

"Strategic adjustments," Elena repeated, her voice dripping with sarcasm. "That's one way to describe embezzlement."

Marcus rubbed his temples, exhaustion evident in his posture. "It's not enough to bring them down," he said. "But it's a start."

"So, what's our next move?" Jacob asked, looking between them.

"We take this to the press," Elena said firmly. "If the board won't act, public pressure will force their hand."

Marcus hesitated. "Going public is risky. If we don't present this carefully, it could backfire."

"Then we make sure it's airtight," Elena replied. "This hospital deserves better, Marcus. And so do you."

Victoria's Intervention

Victoria Langston's office was quiet; the usual hum of the hospital muted under the weight of her conversation with Richard Hayes. He paced the room, agitation evident in every step.

"They have recordings," Hayes snapped. "If this gets out, we're finished."

Victoria leaned back in her chair, her expression calm but unreadable. "Calm down, Richard. Panic doesn't solve problems."

"You really think this is something we can spin?" he asked incredulously. "They have us on tape discussing the funds."

"They don't have context," Victoria said smoothly. "We've faced worse. This hospital is resilient, and so are we."

"You're too calm about this," Hayes muttered, running a hand through his hair. "If this gets out, it's your reputation on the line too."

Victoria's gaze hardened. "And that's exactly why it won't get out. Trust me, Richard. I'll handle this."

Elena and Marcus Confront Victoria

Later that afternoon, Marcus and Elena stood outside Victoria's office, tension thick in the air. Marcus hesitated before knocking.

"Are you sure about this?" Elena asked.

"No," Marcus admitted. "But it's the right thing to do."

The door opened, and Victoria's sharp gaze fixed on them.

"Dr. Rainer. Nurse Martinez. What brings you here?"

Marcus stepped inside, his expression firm.

"We need to talk."

Victoria gestured toward the chairs in front of her desk.

"By all means," she said.

Elena crossed her arms, choosing to remain standing. "We know about the funds," she said bluntly. "And we know you're involved."

Victoria's expression remained steady, almost serene. "That's a serious accusation, Nurse Martinez. I hope you have proof to back it up."

"We do," Marcus said, his voice unwavering. "And we're giving you a chance to come clean before this goes public."

For the first time, Victoria's composure faltered—a flicker of anger flashing in her eyes. "You have no idea what you're getting into," she said coldly. "This isn't just about St. Victoria. You're playing a dangerous game, and if you're not careful, you'll get burned."

"We're not the ones who should be worried," Elena shot back. "The truth is coming out, whether you like it or not."

Later that afternoon, Marcus and Elena stood outside Victoria's office. The tension between them was thick, almost tangible. Marcus hesitated before knocking, his hand hovering over the polished wood.

The Antagonist's Move

In a dimly lit office across town, the orchestrator of the corruption sat at their desk, fingers flying over the keyboard. Lines of code streamed across the monitor as they worked to erase every trace that could lead back to them.

The phone buzzed. The antagonist answered, voice sharp and controlled.

"What is it?"

"They're going public," came the tense reply. "We need to act fast."

"I already have," the antagonist said. "By the time they finish, there'll be nothing left to find."

They ended the call and stared at the screen for a moment before pressing one final key. The monitor went black—evidence gone, silence settling in its place.

Closing Scene

That evening, Marcus, Elena, and Jacob gathered in the hospital's break room. Despite the exhaustion in their faces, their resolve held firm against what lay ahead.

"They're going to fight back," Jacob said. "Hard."

"Let them," Elena replied. "We're not backing down."

Marcus nodded, steady and sure. "Whatever it takes, we'll see this through."

Outside, the city lights shimmered against the night sky—a quiet reminder that even in darkness, hope can still find a way to shine.

CHAPTER 12

The Escalation

The tension at St. Victoria Medical Center hung in the air as dawn broke. Marcus Rainer stood outside the hospital; the crisp morning breeze did little to calm the storm inside him. The confrontation with Victoria Langston had shaken him, but it hadn't broken him. Today was a new day — they had to move forward.

Inside, Elena Martinez and Jacob Wyatt were already in the staff lounge, a laptop open on the table as they ran through the findings again. Each document and recording felt like another part of a puzzle they were racing to finish.

"Anything new?" Marcus asked as he stepped in, shrugging off his coat.

Jacob shook his head. "No smoking gun yet, but we're getting closer. If we can trace the offshore account to someone on the board, it's over for them."

"And if we can't?" Marcus asked.

"Then we find another way," Elena said. "We're not stopping now."

Victoria's Countermove

In her office, Victoria Langston paced with the phone pressed to her ear. Her usual composure was fraying as she spoke in low, urgent tones.

"They're digging too deep," she said. "If this keeps up, it won't stop with the board. It will reach all of us."

The voice on the other end stayed calm and measured. "Then make it stop. You have the authority to neutralize the situation."

Victoria halted, eyes narrowing. "Neutralize? What exactly are you suggesting?"

"Do what's necessary," the voice replied. "Before it's too late."

She ended the call and stood very still for a moment, the weight of the choice pressing down. Reaching for a folder on her desk, her fingers hovered over the hospital logo stamped on the cover. Whatever she decided next would have consequences far beyond St. Victoria.

A Shocking Revelation

Later that afternoon, Marcus, Elena, and Jacob met in a small conference room tucked away from the main hall. Elena opened a file on her laptop, her expression tense.

"I found something," she said, turning the screen toward them. "It's an email chain between Victoria and Richard Hayes. They've been coordinating transfers to the offshore account."

Marcus leaned forward, scanning the emails. His eyes widened. "This ties them directly to the corruption."

"It gets worse," Elena said. She switched to another document, revealing a spreadsheet of transactions. "The money isn't vanishing—it's being funneled into a private research facility owned by one of the board members."

Jacob stared at the screen. "They're stealing from the hospital to fill their own accounts."

"And risking patient safety in the process," Marcus said, his voice tight. "This is it. This is the proof we've been waiting for."

The Antagonist Strikes Back

As the trio finalized their plan to present the evidence, an alarm shattered the quiet of the hospital. The PA system crackled, and a voice rang out: "Code Black. All personnel, initiate emergency protocols."

Jacob shot to his feet. "What's happening?"

Marcus's phone vibrated. An unknown number flashed on the screen, followed by a single message that sent a chill through him.

Message: This is your last warning. Back off.

He showed the message to Elena, whose face hardened. "They're trying to scare us."

"It's more than that," Marcus said. "They're making their move."

Chaos in the Hospital

Emergency protocols sent staff scrambling. Patients were moved to safe zones, and a heavy tension settled over the ward. Marcus, Elena, and Jacob threaded their way through the chaos, determination unchanged despite the obstacles.

"We need to get this to the press before they bury it," Marcus said as they headed for the hospital's media room.

When they reached it, the door was locked and a "Maintenance in Progress" sign was taped to the glass. From inside came the faint, mechanical hum of a server being wiped clean.

"They're erasing everything," Jacob said, urgency cutting through his voice.

"Not if we stop them." Elena grabbed a fire extinguisher from the wall, smashed the glass case, and reached in to unlatch the door.

A Race Against Time

Inside the media room, a lone figure sat hunched at a computer, fingers flying across the keyboard. They spun around as Marcus, Elena, and Jacob burst in, surprise flashing across their face.

"Step away from the computer," Marcus ordered, his voice steady and commanding.

The figure hesitated, then smirked. "You're too late. The files are gone."

"Not all of them," Elena said, holding up a flash drive. "We made copies."

The smirk vanished, replaced by sudden fury. The figure lunged, reaching for the drive, but Jacob moved fast, blocking their path. A brief struggle followed before the intruder broke free and bolted into the hallway, vanishing into the chaos beyond.

Marcus turned to Elena, his chest rising with relief. "Let's finish this."

Closing Scene

Later that night, the trio sat in Marcus's apartment, the flash drive plugged into a laptop. The screen displayed their evidence: a damning collection of emails, financial records, and recorded conversations.

"We take this to the press first thing in the morning," Marcus said, voice resolute.

"And then what?" Jacob asked.

Elena's gaze was steady. "Then we fight. No matter what it takes."

Outside, the city was quiet—a calm before the storm about to break.

CHAPTER 13

The Exposure

The early morning light cast a pale glow over the city as Marcus Rainer, Elena Martinez, and Jacob Wyatt approached the local newsroom. They had spent the night preparing, their evidence carefully organized. This was the moment to reveal the truth.

Inside, the newsroom buzzed with activity. Phones rang, reporters shouted across desks, and the scent of stale coffee hung in the air. The trio approached the front desk, where a receptionist watched them with curiosity.

"Can I help you?" she asked.

"We need to speak with a reporter," Marcus said. "We have information about corruption at St. Victoria Medical Center."

The receptionist's eyes widened. "One moment," she said, picking up the phone.

Within minutes, they were led to a small conference room. A journalist with sharp eyes and a notepad waited.

"I'm Sarah Bennett," she said, motioning for them to sit. "Tell me everything."

Laying It All Out

Elena took the lead, opening her laptop and projecting the flash drive's contents onto the screen.

"This is a collection of emails, financial records, and recordings," she began. "It proves that members of the St. Victoria board—including Victoria Langston and Richard Hayes—have been siphoning hospital funds into offshore accounts."

Sarah's pen flew across her notepad. "And the money? Where has it been going?"

"A private research facility owned by one of the board members," Jacob said. "They're using hospital resources to fund personal projects, leaving patients and staff to suffer the consequences."

Marcus leaned forward, his voice steady. "This corruption isn't just financial. Lives have been put at risk. Patients were endangered because resources meant for their care were diverted."

Sarah's gaze sharpened. "Do you have names?"

"Yes," Elena said, clicking to a document listing key players. "And we're prepared to testify if necessary."

The Breaking Story

Within hours, the newsroom buzzed with activity. Cameras were set up, anchors prepared for the evening broadcast, and phones rang constantly as reporters reached out to board members for comment.

Back at the hospital, the atmosphere was tense. Staff huddled in small groups, their conversations hushed but urgent. The news was already leaking, and everyone sensed that something major was about to happen.

Victoria Langston sat in her office, her calm facade starting to crack. Her phone buzzed relentlessly with messages, each one more frantic than the last. She ignored them, her mind racing for a way to regain control.

The Broadcast

That evening, the team gathered at Marcus's apartment to watch the broadcast. The air was thick with anticipation as the anchor's face appeared on the screen.

"Good evening," the anchor began. "Tonight, we bring you an exclusive report on allegations of corruption at St. Victoria Medical Center. Our investigation reveals evidence of financial misconduct involving senior board members and the misallocation of hospital funds."

As the report played, the trio exchanged glances, their expressions a mix of relief and apprehension. The evidence was damning, and the names of those involved were read aloud for the city to hear.

The Fallout

The next morning, the hospital was in chaos. Reporters swarmed the entrance, cameras flashing as they shouted questions at anyone who passed by. Inside, staff whispered nervously, uncertain what the day—and the headlines—would bring.

Victoria Langston's office was empty, her desk cleared out overnight. Richard Hayes was nowhere to be found. The remaining board members scrambled to contain the fallout, issuing a statement promising a full investigation.

Marcus stood in the hallway, watching the commotion unfold. Elena approached him, her expression tired but determined.

"We did it," she said.

"For now," Marcus replied. "But this is just the beginning. There's a lot of rebuilding to do."

Closing Scene

As the day drew to a close, Marcus, Elena, and Jacob stood outside the hospital, the setting sun casting a warm glow over the building. For the first time in weeks, a sense of calm settled over them.

"So, what now?" Jacob asked.

"We keep fighting," Elena said. "For the staff, for the patients, for everything this hospital stands for."

Marcus nodded, a faint smile on his face. "And we make sure this never happens again."

The three stood together, the weight of their journey still heavy but now shared. They had exposed the corruption, but the road ahead remained long. Together, they were ready to face it.

CHAPTER 14
Rebuilding Trust

The days following the broadcast were a whirlwind at St. Victoria Medical Center. The exposed corruption had left a deep wound in the hospital's reputation, and the remaining leadership scrambled to stabilize operations. Staff meetings were held daily, updates streamed in from investigative teams, and a new interim board was quickly assembled to manage the fallout.

Marcus Rainer stood in the atrium, watching nurses, doctors, and administrators move with purpose. The uncertainty that had gripped them for weeks was giving way to cautious determination. Elena Martinez approached, clipboard in hand, her expression resolute.

"They're holding another staff meeting in Conference Room B," she said. "The interim board wants to address everyone's concerns."

Marcus nodded. "How's the morale?"

"Better than I expected," Elena admitted. "But there's still fear. People are wondering whom they can trust."

"We'll have to earn that trust back," Marcus said firmly. "And it starts today."

The Staff Meeting

The conference room was packed, every seat filled and others pressed against the walls. At the front stood members of the interim board, joined by Marcus, Elena, and Jacob Wyatt. A hush fell over the crowd as the meeting began.

"First, we want to acknowledge the courage of those who brought these issues to light," one of the board members said, nodding toward Marcus, Elena, and Jacob. "Their actions have put us on a path toward accountability and transparency."

A ripple of applause ran through the room, tinged with apprehension. Marcus stepped forward, his gaze sweeping across the crowd.

"I know many of you are angry, hurt, and uncertain about what comes next," he began. "I don't blame you. This hospital has been through hell, and rebuilding it won't be easy. But I believe in this place, and I believe in all of you. Together, we can restore St. Victoria to what it was meant to be."

Elena followed, her voice steady. "This is our chance to set things right. To create a culture where every voice matters, where patient care always comes first. But it will take all of us working together."

A Plan for the Future

Over the next few days, task forces were established to tackle specific challenges: financial recovery, patient safety, staff morale, and communication. Marcus took charge of the financial recovery team, working closely with the interim board to trace and recover misappropriated funds.

Elena led the patient safety team, implementing stricter protocols and making sure resources were properly allocated. Jacob, meanwhile, focused on staff morale, organizing open forums where employees could share concerns and offer suggestions.

"It's amazing how much people want to help," Jacob said during one meeting. "They just needed someone to listen."

Marcus smiled faintly. "That's the heart of this place. The people."

Victoria's Reckoning

While the hospital worked to rebuild, Victoria Langston's world was falling apart. Investigators had uncovered more damning evidence, and she now faced multiple charges, including embezzlement and endangering patients. Her once-commanding presence had been reduced to headlines on every news outlet.

Marcus watched the coverage from his office, relief and sadness washing over him. Victoria had been a formidable force, and though her actions were inexcusable, he couldn't help but wonder what had driven her to such extremes.

"Justice is justice," Elena said as she stepped into the room. "She made her choices, and now she'll face the consequences."

Marcus nodded. "I just hope this sends a message. We can't afford to let something like this happen again."

Closing Scene

A week later, the hospital atrium was filled with staff, patients, and local supporters attending a community event celebrating the hospital's new direction. Marcus stood at the podium, flanked by Elena and Jacob, addressing the crowd.

"Today marks the start of a new chapter for St. Victoria," he said. "This hospital has always been more than just a building. It represents hope, healing, and resilience. Together, we'll honor that legacy and build a future we can all be proud of."

The audience erupted into applause, and for the first time in months, optimism hung in the air. As Marcus stepped down from the podium, he glanced at Elena and Jacob.

"We did it," he said.

"No," Elena replied with a smile. "We're just getting started."

The next week at St. Victoria wasn't healing—it was triage.

CHAPTER 15

The Turning Point

The morning light filtered through the tall windows of St. Victoria Medical Center's atrium, casting soft rays onto the bustling floor below. The hospital had a pulse again, steady and strong. Marcus Rainer stood at the top of the grand staircase, watching the activity with a renewed sense of purpose. For the first time in months, he felt hope—not just for the hospital, but for himself.

Elena Martinez approached, tablet in hand, a knowing smile on her face. "I've got good news," she said. "The financial recovery task force has already traced half of the misappropriated funds. They've started reallocating them to critical departments."

"That's a start," Marcus said, his gaze sweeping over the atrium. "How's morale?"

"Better," Elena replied. "But there's still unease. Trust takes time to rebuild."

Marcus nodded. "Then we keep working."

The Board's Decision

Later that day, Marcus and Elena sat in the conference room with the interim board. Jacob Wyatt joined them, his usual nervous energy tempered by determination.

"Dr. Rainer, Nurse Martinez, Mr. Wyatt," the interim chair began, "I want to commend you for your courage and perseverance. This hospital owes you a great deal."

"Thank you," Marcus replied. "But the real work is just beginning. We need to ensure the changes we're implementing last."

The chair nodded. "Agreed. The board has approved a new set of oversight measures to prevent future misconduct. We've also decided to formalize the leadership roles you've taken on. Dr. Rainer, we'd like you to step in as acting chief administrator."

Marcus's eyes widened slightly, and he exchanged a glance with Elena and Jacob.

"It's a lot of responsibility," he said carefully. "But if it means I can help rebuild this hospital, I'm in."

Healing Wounds

Over the next few weeks, the changes began to take hold. Departments that had suffered from underfunding saw a resurgence as resources were restored, and new protocols ensured transparency and accountability at every level.

Elena led a mentorship program for nurses, focusing on leadership and patient advocacy, while Jacob's open forums continued to thrive, fostering a strong sense of community among the staff.

One afternoon, Marcus visited the pediatric wing, where the laughter of children filled the halls. He paused outside a room where a young boy was drawing with crayons.

"Hi there," Marcus said, crouching down. "What's your name?"

"Alex," the boy replied, holding up a drawing of a superhero. "This is my dad. He's my hero."

Marcus's chest tightened. He thought of Daniel, his own son, and the letter he had written years ago. "That's a wonderful drawing, Alex," he said with a smile. "Your dad must be very proud of you."

Victoria's Final Move

In a courtroom across town, Victoria Langston faced the consequences of her actions. The trial had drawn intense media attention, and the evidence against her was overwhelming. As the verdict was announced, she maintained her composure, though her eyes revealed a brief flicker of regret.

Outside the courthouse, reporters surrounded Marcus, who had attended the trial as a representative of St. Victoria.

"Dr. Rainer, do you feel justice has been served?" one reporter asked.

Marcus paused, choosing his words carefully. "Justice is about accountability," he said. "But it's also about learning from the past to build a better future. That's what we're focused on at St. Victoria."

Closing Scene

That evening, Marcus, Elena, and Jacob stood on the hospital roof, gazing out over the city. The lights of St. Victoria glowed below, a beacon of hope against the darkness.

"We've come a long way," Elena said softly.

"And we still have a long way to go," Jacob added.

"One step at a time," Marcus replied. He pulled Daniel's letter from his pocket, holding it briefly before tucking it away. "For him. For all of them."

Above them, the first stars of the evening began to twinkle. The journey had been arduous, but St. Victoria was alive again, its pulse steady and strong.

CHAPTER 16

Confrontation

Marcus hesitated outside the office door, his breath visible in the cold, air-conditioned hallway. The folder of damning evidence felt heavy in his hands—not from its physical weight, but from the consequences it carried. His heart thudded loudly, and for a moment, he considered walking away. Then Elena's voice came through the earpiece.

"Stay calm. You've got this," she said, steady and reassuring.

He nodded to himself, though no one could see it, and pushed the door open. Inside, the dimly lit office contrasted sharply with the hospital's sterile brightness. The board member leaned back behind a large mahogany desk, a smirk playing on their lips.

"Dr. Rainer," the board member greeted, their tone smooth and measured. "I didn't expect you to come alone. Bold move."

Marcus stepped forward, keeping his expression neutral. He placed the folder on the desk with deliberate care; his eyes fixed on theirs. "I'm giving you a chance to end this quietly—before it gets worse for everyone."

The board member leaned forward, fingers brushing the edge of the folder. They opened it, scanning the contents with a faint chuckle.

"You think this is enough to bring me down?" they asked, raising an eyebrow. "It's impressive, I'll give you that. But it's incomplete. Without context, it's meaningless."

Marcus clenched his fists, forcing his tone steady. "Context won't matter once the press gets hold of it."

"Oh, Marcus," the board member said, shaking their head. They closed the folder and leaned closer, their voice dropping to a chilling whisper. "You think the press will care about your story? About your heroics? No. They'll care about your mistakes. Your addiction. Your negligence. You'll be the headline, not me."

Through the earpiece, Elena's voice came again, firmer this time. "Don't take the bait."

Marcus forced his hands to relax and met the board member's gaze. "Maybe. But at least I'll go down knowing I did the right thing. Can you say the same?"

The board member rose, their presence imposing as they loomed over the desk. "If you release this," they said, voice like ice, "you won't just lose your career. You'll lose everything—family, friends, and your reputation. Gone. Are you ready for that?"

A vibration in Marcus's pocket interrupted the tense moment. He fished out his phone and glanced at the screen:

Elena: GET OUT. NOW.

He gave the board member a faint smile as he pocketed the phone and picked up the folder. "This isn't over," he said evenly. "You'll regret underestimating me."

The board member smirked, watching him head for the door. "I look forward to it."

EPILOGUE

The Aftermath

The winter sun shone weakly over St. Victoria Medical Center, casting long shadows across the parking lot where a line of media vans had claimed residence. Reporters milled around, microphones in hand, waiting for the next statement or scandal.

Inside the hospital, the atmosphere was no less fraught. Staff bustled about, their movements quick and tense, as if trying to outrun the chaos still rippling through their workplace.

Marcus's Reflection

Marcus sat on a park bench across the street; a steaming cup of coffee cradled in his hands. His eyes scanned the building, resting on the busy main entrance where nurses wheeled patients in and out, oblivious to the drama unfolding around them. Despite the city's noise, the world around him felt silent.

It's strange how life goes on, he thought. Even when everything has fallen apart.

His phone buzzed in his pocket, pulling him out of the reverie. He glanced at the screen and saw Elena's name.

Message: Meeting at 3. We'll need your input. Don't be late.

A faint smile tugged at his lips. Tossing the now-empty coffee cup into a nearby bin, he stood and started walking toward the hospital, each step a little lighter than the last.

Elena's Commitment

In the nurses' lounge, Elena sifted through patient files, her fingers moving methodically across the pages. The familiar hum of the hospital wrapped around her, a steadying presence amid the chaos. Her shoulders stiffened slightly as Jacob entered, a clipboard tucked under his arm.

"You ready for this?" Jacob asked.

Elena exhaled, a hint of tension in her breath. "As ready as I'll ever be. You?"

"Not really. But someone has to step up, right?" Jacob replied.

A small smile softened Elena's expression. She patted his shoulder, her voice steady. "You're doing well, Jacob. Just don't lose yourself in the process."

Jacob grinned. "Don't worry about me. I've got this."

Victoria's Quiet Maneuvering

Across the city, Victoria Langston reclined in a leather armchair in her luxurious apartment. The muted voice of a news anchor filtered through the room as she scanned documents on her tablet.

"The removal of a key board member marks a turning point for St. Victoria Medical Center. But questions remain about the hospital's future," the anchor reported.

Victoria's lips curled into a faint smirk. She muted the television and picked up her phone, dialing with practiced precision.

"Prepare the proposal. We'll be ready to make our move soon," she said, her voice calm and resolute, as if the storm engulfing the hospital barely touched her. She leaned back in the chair, a glass of wine glinting in the dim light.

A Fresh Start

The afternoon sun glinted off a new sign being installed above the hospital's main entrance, the bright letters marking a fresh chapter for St. Victoria Medical Center. Marcus, Elena, and Jacob stood together on the sidewalk, watching the workers finish the installation. The air felt lighter, charged with the promise of change.

"Think this will make a difference?" Elena asked.

"It's a start," Marcus replied.

Jacob smiled. "We'll make sure it does."

As they turned to re-enter the hospital, a shadowy figure lingered across the street, half-hidden by the fading light. Their expression was unreadable, their stance still as they watched the trio disappear into the building. A soft click echoed as the figure ended a phone call, the sound quickly swallowed by the city's din.

Later, Marcus entered the rival board member's office with the folder in hand, but the atmosphere felt different this time. Charged. Electric.

He wasn't imagining it. Someone else was there.

A second cup of coffee sat on the desk. A jacket draped over a spare chair. Fresh footprints on the polished floor.

"You came alone," the board member said. "Braver than I expected."

Marcus set the folder down slowly. "You're done hiding behind money and threats."

"Oh, Marcus, " The board member's whisper sent ice down his spine. "You still don't understand. I'm not the one you should be afraid of."

Before he could respond, a faint click sounded from behind the wall—like someone unplugging a device.

Then a voice came over the intercom: "He wasn't supposed to come alone."

Marcus froze. The board member froze.

Elena's voice suddenly buzzed through his earpiece, frantic: "Marcus—don't turn around. Someone's in the room with you."

His pulse hammered in his ears. Behind him, breath slow, controlled, exhaled softly. He wasn't alone. He spun. No one was there, but the window was open. Curtains shifting. Night air cold. And a faint, unmistakable scent lingering in the room, citrus and smoke.

A signature scent. The same scent from the hospital stairwell weeks ago.

The presence had vanished—but not before a whisper brushed the air: "Book two, Marcus. Let's see if you make it there."

Marcus grabbed the folder and ran.

Elena's voice shouted through his earpiece, "They're coming after you!"

As Marcus reached the hallway, alarms erupted. Security sprinted past. Lights flickered. Hospital computers rebooted on their own.

A full assault was underway. And the enemy wasn't hiding anymore.

ABOUT THE AUTHOR

Tonya Jones is an author, nurse, veteran, and advocate whose life's work has been shaped by compassion, resilience, and a fierce devotion to truth. Born and raised in Sterlington, Louisiana, and now residing in Cedar Hill, Texas, Tonya brings more than fifteen years of medical experience as both a nurse and former Hospital Corpsman in the U.S. Navy to the heart pounding world of *The Silent Pulse: Whispers of Deceit*.

Her writing is deeply influenced by her real-life journey through profound loss and extraordinary strength. Tonya is the mother of Deterrious "DJ" Jones, whose passing transformed her mission and ignited her dedication to mental health awareness, suicide prevention, and breaking generational silence. In loving honor of DJ, Tonya and her family participate every year in the Out of the Darkness Walk, raising funds and awareness to support prevention, healing, and hope. Her grandson, Terrion, DJ's son, remains one of her greatest joys and inspirations.

Tonya is also the author of *Breaking the Silence: A Mother's Journey Through Loss and Advocacy* and *Facing Tomorrow: A Woman's Journey of Hope and Healing*, two powerful works that illuminate the emotional landscape of grief, faith, and rebuilding after heartbreak. Her next release, *The Silent Pulse*, marks her expansion into dramatic, suspense driven fiction: stories laced with secrets, high stakes, and the quiet betrayals that pulse beneath the surface of everyday life.

Beyond the page, Tonya finds fulfillment in uplifting others, sharing her testimony, and using her voice to create change. She credits her strength, creativity, and continued purpose to God's grace and to the unwavering love of her family. Every story she writes is rooted in legacy, carried by faith, and dedicated to the people who shaped her journey.

All praise and glory to God because without Him and without her family's love, none of this would be possible.

ACKNOWLEDGEMENTS

First and foremost, I give all praise, honor, and glory to God, my strength, my peace, and my constant source of grace. Without Him, none of this would be possible. Every word I write and every life I touch is a reflection of His love working through me.

To my beloved son, DJ, your spirit continues to inspire me every single day. You are the heartbeat behind my purpose and the reason I continue to speak, write, and share hope with the world.

To my precious grandson, Terrion, you are a living reminder that love never dies. Your laughter, courage, and light bring me joy beyond words. May you always know how proud your father would be of you.

To my family, thank you for standing by me through every season of this journey. Your prayers, love, and encouragement have carried me through moments when I didn't think I could keep going. You are my foundation, and I am forever grateful for each of you.

To my friends and supporters, thank you for believing in my message, sharing my story, and helping me turn pain into purpose. Your compassion and faith remind me that healing is possible when hearts come together.

To every reader who picks up this book, thank you. Whether you came for the story, the emotion, or the truth behind the fiction, I pray it touches your heart and reminds you that even in silence, there is strength... and in every pulse, there is purpose.